Treasure in
Trident City

★ Also by ★
Debbie Dadey

MERMAID TALES

Coming Soon

Mermaid Tales

★ Debbie Dadey ★

BOOK 8

Illustrated by
Tatevik Avakyan

Treasure in Trident City

ALADDIN

NEW YORK   LONDON   TORONTO   SYDNEY   NEW DELHI

ALADDIN

An imprint of Simon & Schuster Children's Publishing Division

1230 Avenue of the Americas, New York, NY 10020

First Aladdin paperback edition May 2014

Text copyright © 2014 by Debbie Dadey

Illustrations copyright © 2014 by Tatevik Avakyan

Book design by Karin Paprocki

All rights reserved, including the right of reproduction in whole or in part in any form.

ALADDIN is a trademark of Simon & Schuster, Inc.,

and related logo is a registered trademark of Simon & Schuster, Inc.

Also available in an Aladdin hardcover edition.

For information about special discounts for bulk purchases,

please contact Simon & Schuster Special Sales at 1-866-506-1949

or business@simonandschuster.com.

The Simon & Schuster Speakers Bureau can bring authors to your live event.

For more information or to book an event contact the

Simon & Schuster Speakers Bureau at 1-866-248-3049

or visit our website at www.simonspeakers.com.

The text of this book was set in Belucian Book.

Manufactured in the United States of America 0917 OFF

6 8 10 9 7 5

Library of Congress Control Number 2013019113

ISBN 978-1-4424-8267-8 (hc)

ISBN 978-1-4424-8266-1 (pbk)

ISBN 978-1-4424-8268-5 (eBook)

*In memory of two treasures,
my uncle John Dohr and
my friend Kate DiRugeris*

★ ★ ★ ★

Acknowledgment

Thanks to Ellen Mager at Booktenders' Secret Garden for your dedication to children's literature.

Cast of Characters

Shelly

Echo

Kiki

Pearl

Rocky

Contents

Mirror, Mirror

PEARL SWAMP CURLED THE TIP of her gold tail to make a bow. Then she flipped it out quickly to make a circle. It was hard to do while seated, but just for fun, she began practicing her Tail Flippers dance. Her school, Trident Academy, had a dance and gymnastics group called the Tail Flippers. Pearl was so proud that she'd made the team this year!

"Pearl!" her third-grade teacher, Mrs. Karp, snapped. "Are you paying attention?"

Pearl sat up straight and stared innocently at her teacher. "Of course! I always pay attention to you, Mrs. Karp." Of course, that wasn't *exactly* true. Pearl did *try* to pay attention, but sometimes school was just too boring! She longed for something exciting to happen.

"As I was saying, class," Mrs. Karp continued, "today we will start a storytelling project."

A merboy named Rocky Ridge groaned loud enough for the whole class to hear.

Pearl felt like groaning too. Mrs. Karp was always coming up with new tasks for them, some very dull!

Mrs. Karp frowned at Rocky. "The project will include two assignments. For the first assignment, each of you will choose a story to study. Then you will practice telling it to your family or in front of a mirror. You will share your story with the class tomorrow."

Kiki Coral raised her hand. "What's a mirror?"

"Don't you have a mirror?" Pearl asked in surprise. Even though Kiki was from far-off waters, Pearl couldn't believe she didn't know what a mirror was!

Kiki shook her head. Most of the other third graders shrugged, so Shelly Siren explained, "It's a piece of glass that you look in to see yourself. What you see is called a reflection. A lot of humans have them."

Pearl sniffed, tossing her long blond hair behind her shoulders. Shelly was such a know-it-all. Just because she lived with her grandfather in an apartment above the People Museum, she thought she was an expert on *all* human things. "My family has ten of them," Pearl bragged.

"No one has ten mirrors in their shell," Rocky scoffed.

Pearl lifted her pointy nose up in the water. "Well, *we* do! If you don't believe me, you can come over and see for yourself!"

Rocky made a face. "A giant octopus couldn't drag me to your shell."

★ 4 ★

"That's quite enough," Mrs. Karp said sharply. "If you don't have a mirror, you may practice with a friend."

A mergirl named Echo Reef raised her hand and asked, "What's the second part of the storytelling project?"

Mrs. Karp peered over her glasses and smiled at Echo. "Thank you for asking. The second assignment will be to make up your own story and tell it to the class."

"That's more like it." Rocky grinned, sitting back in his sponge seat. "I'm good at making up stories."

Pearl knew that was true. Rocky was always making up tales, and they were usually great big fat lies. But even Pearl had to admit she liked the idea of being in front of the class and telling a story she made up. She could say almost anything! Plus, Pearl loved it when everyone looked at her. It made her feel so special.

Mrs. Karp thumped her white tail on her desk to get everyone's attention. "It's time to head to the library to choose the stories for your first assignment." The merkids floated down the hall. Pearl wasn't eager to find a story among all the rock and seaweed books, but she did love looking at the beautiful domed library ceiling. It was made of glistening mother-of-pearl, and its fancy chandeliers sparkled with glowing jellyfish. If the whole school was as pretty as the library, Pearl was sure she would like studying more.

Pearl and her friend Wanda Slug sat down at a rock table that was piled high with stories written on pieces of seaweed. "What kind of story do you want to find?" Wanda asked. "I'd love one about a princess!"

Pearl scrunched her nose. "A princess would be all right, I guess," she said. "But only if it's *really* exciting."

Just then there was a loud yelp across the room. "No wavy way!" Rocky yelled. "Look what I found!"

2

Story Time!

ALMOST THE ENTIRE CLASS gathered around Rocky. "I found a story about a pirate treasure!" he exclaimed.

"Pirates are cool," a merboy named Adam said, peering over Rocky's shoulder.

"That's not even the best part!" Rocky

boasted. "The treasure is right here in Trident City!"

Pearl floated over to Rocky as the other merkids giggled in excitement. After all, Trident Academy was located in the middle of Trident City. The treasure couldn't be too far away.

"It's just a pretend story from a book," Shelly said. "There's not really a treasure."

"But what if it's not made up?" Rocky protested. "What if it's real?"

Pearl squeezed in next to Rocky. Her eyes grew wide as she scanned the story, which included a faded drawing of an old, abandoned pirate ship. "It says there are diamonds as big as a merman's fist and rubies large enough to choke a shark!"

Rocky nodded. "And they're all hidden inside a treasure chest that's haunted by pirate ghosts."

"Ghosts?" Echo Reef shuddered. "Ghosts are creepy."

Shelly shook her head. "Ghosts aren't real."

Rocky pointed his brown tail at Shelly. "How do you know?"

"Yeah," Pearl said, rolling her big green eyes. "Ghosts are supposed to be invisible. For all you know, they're floating all over this library." Pearl didn't believe in ghosts, but she hated when Shelly acted like she knew everything.

Echo looked around as if she expected a ghost to jump out at any moment.

"I know," Shelly said. "I just don't believe in them."

"Who cares about pirates or ghosts anyway?" Pearl said. "I want to know where to find that treasure!"

Rocky continued to read the story aloud. "This doesn't say exactly where the treasure is, but you wouldn't want to go near it. The pirate ghosts guard it! There's no telling what they'd do to you if you tried to take it."

Just then the librarian, Miss Scylla, swam over with one eyebrow raised. "What's all the fuss about? Have you finished choosing your stories?" Everyone sighed and got back to work.

But Pearl couldn't stop thinking about

how thrilling it would be to find a real pirate's treasure. She'd probably even get her picture in the *Trident City Tide*, the local newsweed. She closed her eyes, imagining the headline:

BEAUTIFUL YOUNG MERMAID
FINDS TREASURE

THAT NIGHT AT DINNER, PEARL ASKED her parents if they'd heard about the treasure in Trident City. "That's just a silly old legend," Mrs. Swamp said, wiping her mouth with a napkin.

"Actually," began Mr. Swamp, putting his glass of comb jelly tea down on the marble table, "I've seen the ship. It's beyond

Whale Mountain and the Big Volcano."
Whale Mountain was a big underwater
mountain shaped like the hump on a
whale's back.

Pearl slapped the table gleefully. "I knew
it!" She couldn't wait to tell that know-it-
all Shelly that the treasure *was* real.

"But the ship is haunted," her dad said
in a quiet voice.

Her mom laughed. "Don't be silly!
There's no such thing as a haunted ship."

Her dad raised his eyebrows, picking up
his glass. "Maybe not, but there's something
spooky about that ship. Frank at work told
me he swam by there one day and heard
ghosts moaning. He said that over the
years many merpeople have disappeared

into that ship and never been seen again."

Pearl's mom sighed. "You know Frank likes to make things up."

"It doesn't matter," Pearl's father said. "Merfolk stay away from it anyway, because the ship's wood is rotting. It's so old that the whole place is dangerous."

Pearl nodded and took another sip of her cuttlefish chowder. All she could think about was a big treasure chest full of diamonds and rubies.

Deep-Sea Jewels

SWEET SEAWEED! WHAT ARE YOU swearing?" Pearl asked Rocky the next morning. They were in their classroom at Trident Academy, and all the third graders were staring at Rocky.

Rocky had a pirate hat on his head. He

wore a necklace of bootlace worms and an acorn barnacle eye patch. A ferocious-looking black dragonfish was wound around his tummy for a belt, and a long needlefish stuck out of the belt. Rocky grinned. "I'm a pirate, just like in the story I found! Mrs. Karp should give me extra points for this getup."

Pearl pointed at Rocky and smirked. "You look silly!" Her blond hair swirled around her as she slid into her desk, secretly wishing she had thought to wear a costume. She had a tiara at home that would have gone perfectly with the princess story she'd found in the library yesterday.

"All right, class," Mrs. Karp said as she floated into the room. "Let's get to"—she paused when she saw Rocky, but quickly continued—"work. Miss Scylla told me you had quite a lively discussion about pirate treasure in the library yesterday. So I thought we would have a quick lesson on deep-sea jewels before you share the stories you found."

Pearl's ears perked up at the word "jewels." She excitedly twisted her pearl necklace between her fingers as Mrs. Karp continued. "As you may know, human pirates sailed the ocean waters hundreds of years ago, stealing from other ships and collecting valuable jewels and gold. Sometimes they buried the jewels so that no one else could find them. There are four jewels that pirates liked best: diamonds, rubies, sapphires, and emeralds."

Pearl frowned, still clutching her necklace. "Didn't they like pearls?" she asked.

Mrs. Karp nodded. "I'm sure they did. But diamonds were their favorite. In fact, you may have seen diamonds around Trident City. They are quite hard, so merfolk often use them to cut doors in shells."

Wanda raised her hand. "Mr. Fangtooth carries a diamond saw sometimes."

"Yes, but pirates collected them for their beauty and value. Diamonds are worth a lot of money to humans, and we merfolk value them too. Diamonds come in many colors: yellow, brown, gray, blue, green, black, pink, violet, orange, purple, and red. Our historical records show that pirates liked the clear ones best."

Mrs. Karp opened a wooden box and took out a shiny object. "In fact, I've brought a diamond for you to see. Please be careful when you handle it." She looked directly at Rocky as she said, "Remember, they are very valuable!"

Mrs. Karp passed the diamond to Echo. It was bigger than her hand and a sparkling yellow color. Pearl could hardly wait to hold it.

Next their teacher held up a glittering scarlet stone. "This is a ruby. They're almost as hard as diamonds, and they are always red." She passed the stone to Wanda.

According to Mrs. Karp, emeralds were very rare and valuable, and transparent blue sapphires made up the windows in King Neptune's castle. It was all very exciting, but Pearl could barely pay attention.

Her eyes never left the diamond. Finally it was her turn to hold it!

Pearl lifted the shining jewel to her face and sighed in delight. She could see her reflection about a hundred times in all its different surfaces! She'd never seen anything sparkle quite so much.

Right then and there, Pearl decided that she was going to get her very own diamond—no matter what!

A Million Rubies

I THOUGHT OF IT FIRST!" PEARL
snapped.

Wanda shrugged in her seat next
to Pearl in the lunchroom. "That's not
true. Rocky was the one who told us about
the treasure."

Pearl took a sip of her big kelp drink

and frowned. They had spent the morning sharing the stories they'd found in the library. Of course, her story was the best. Then Mrs. Karp had told them that the day after tomorrow they would finish the second part of the storytelling project. They'd each tell a story that they made up themselves. Pearl had decided to make up a pirate story. But what fun would it be if everyone else was doing the same thing?

Just then she had an idea. She knew how to make her story really stand out from the others.

"I'm doing it," Pearl announced to the girls at her table.

"Me too," Wanda agreed. "I just have

to decide what to name my pirate. How about Pierre? Pierre the Pirate."

Pearl crossed her arms. "I'm not talking about pirate stories. I'm talking about finding a real pirate treasure." She waited until she was sure everyone was watching. "Actually, I know where the Trident City treasure is, the one Rocky was talking about yesterday. My dad told me."

"Y-you do?" a girl named Morgan asked.

"Yes, and I'm going to find it after school tomorrow," Pearl told the girls. She could tell they were impressed.

Echo floated past the table and glanced at Pearl. "Find what?" Echo asked.

"The pirate's treasure!" Pearl announced loudly.

"Are you crazy?" Echo said. "Ghosts guard it!"

Pearl shrugged. She didn't believe in ghosts, and she certainly wasn't going to let some old legend keep her from a chest full of jewels—not to mention having the very best story to tell the class tomorrow. "If someone wants to go with me," she added, "I'll let them have one ruby."

"I've always wanted to find a pirate's treasure," Echo admitted. "But I wouldn't go on a haunted ship for a million rubies!"

"I would!" Rocky said with a grin. He floated up beside Echo, still wearing his pirate getup.

"I thought you were scared of ghosts," Echo told Rocky.

Rocky shrugged. "Last night my dad told me there's no such thing. And he should know—he's the mayor of Trident City."

"Don't go," Wanda warned. "It's dangerous."

"And I bet it's against the rules," Echo added.

"What rules?" Pearl asked.

"I don't know," Echo said, "but I'm sure there's a rule against it somewhere."

Pearl rolled her eyes. Who cared about rules? Rules were boring!

Suddenly she couldn't wait for tomorrow. She wished she didn't have Tail Flippers practice after school; otherwise she'd go right away. She was going to find that treasure, no matter what.

Haunted?

THE NEXT AFTERNOON PEARL and Rocky raced out of Trident Academy as soon as the last conch sounded. "This is such a thrill!" Pearl exclaimed. She couldn't believe she was going on a real treasure hunt.

"I even brought my pirate costume, just in case we run into anything fishy," Rocky added, pulling the costume and needlefish from behind a rock. In just a few minutes he had the costume on, with the needlefish in his belt.

Pearl could care less about silly costumes; she just wanted to find the treasure!

"Wait!" Echo called from the school doorway. "Don't go!"

Shelly glided around Echo. "Don't worry," Shelly assured her. "They won't get far."

"Yes, we will," Rocky insisted.

Shelly shook her head. "You'll get scared and come back when you can't find anything."

"You really think so?" Echo asked, looking relieved.

"Of course," Shelly said. Kiki floated beside her and nodded.

"Wait!" Wanda cried as she rushed out the doorway.

"Oh my Neptune!" Pearl complained. "What now?"

"I'm coming with you," Wanda said.

Pearl put her right hand on her right hip and cocked her head. "I thought you were afraid."

Wanda giggled. "I'm terrified, but I don't want to miss the chance to find treasure. I'll go as long as I can have a diamond, plus the ruby you already promised."

"If she gets a diamond, then so do I," Rocky told Pearl.

Pearl let out a giant sigh. She didn't really want to share, but she didn't want to go alone. "All right. You can each have one small diamond, too."

Rocky high-finned the water and Wanda giggled. "This is totally exciting! We're going on a real treasure hunt," she said.

Echo shuddered. "Some excitement is worth missing."

"You're just jealous that you didn't think of finding the treasure first!" Pearl told her before turning to Wanda and Rocky. "Now—let's go find those jewels!"

The three treasure hunters floated away

from the school, leaving Echo, Shelly, and Kiki behind in a swirl of bubbles.

"AHOY, MATIES!" ROCKY CALLED TO A colony of vampire squid as they passed Whale Mountain. But when they reached the Big Volcano at the very edge of Trident City, Rocky looked uncertain. "I've never swum past the Big Volcano," he said with a gulp.

Pearl had been on the Manta Ray Express with her family many times. The enormous manta rays took merpeople anywhere in the ocean for just a couple of shells. But Pearl had never been this far from home all by herself. She was a little afraid, but she wasn't going to let Rocky or Wanda know. "My dad said the ship is close to Whale Mountain, so it shouldn't be much farther," Pearl said confidently. She couldn't remember exactly what her father had said, but she was sure he'd said something about Whale Mountain.

The ocean floor grew darker and darker as they floated away from the city. Pearl was grateful for the light coming from a school of glowing jellyfish, but soon even that light faded. All three merkids gasped as a spiky coffinfish darted between them, nearly slamming into Pearl.

"I think we'd better turn back," Wanda whispered. "We could get really lost out here."

Pearl didn't want to admit it, but she

knew Wanda was right. "Fine," Pearl huffed, whirling around to swim home.

"Wait!" Rocky yelped, pointing straight ahead. "There it is!"

Pearl couldn't believe her eyes. Just beyond a large crop of dead man's fingers, she could make out the murky outline of a huge wooden ship. It looked exactly like the picture from the library, but it was much bigger in real life. And darker.

Wanda whispered like she was afraid ghosts might hear her. "That's the most horrible thing I've ever seen. We should leave. I bet there's a whole bunch of evil ghosts in there."

"Maybe she's right," Rocky said quietly.

Pearl had to admit that it was terrifying.

There was no telling what was inside the mysterious black holes of the rotting ship. She jumped when a blackdevil fish slithered out of one.

Suddenly they heard a sound.

"Oooooooooooooooooohhhhhhhh."

"What was that?" Rocky asked, his eyes as wide as a toadfish's.

"Oooooooooooooooooohhhhhhhh!"

"Oh my Neptune!" Wanda shrieked. "It's a ghost! Swim for it!!"

6

Pirate Ghost

ROCKY AND WANDA ZOOMED off. Although she *was* frightened, Pearl didn't want to let all those jewels slip away. "Don't wimp out now!" she yelled after them. "Let's swim inside and look for the treasure."

"Are you crazy?" Rocky said, screeching to a halt.

"Didn't you hear that—that spooky sound?" Wanda said with a gasp.

"My dad was wrong," Rocky added. "That had to be a ghost!"

Though Pearl was afraid, she hadn't come all this way to get scared off by a little noise. "At least stick around to see if it happens again!"

The merkids waited a few minutes, but they didn't hear anything. Finally Rocky and Wanda agreed to swim back toward the ship. They floated along until they were only about a shell's throw from the hulking vessel. Wreckfish darted in and out of its broken hull. Zoanthid coral covered much of the wood. A harmless goblin shark slithered through the debris.

"Ooooooooooooooooohhhhhhhh!" This time the sound was even louder!

"You call that a little noise?" Rocky shivered. "It sounds like an entire army of pirate ghosts!"

Pearl shook her head to get rid of the idea of pirate ghosts. "I bet it's just the wood creaking," she said bravely, although she wasn't sure anymore. "My dad said the boat is rotting."

"Really?" Wanda squeaked.

Pearl nodded. "Of course. Plus, just think about that treasure! Imagine what you could do with all those diamonds!"

Pearl knew how badly Wanda wanted to be a part of the Tail Flippers even though she hadn't made the team. So Pearl said, "Wanda, I bet they'd put you on the Tail Flippers if you gave diamond necklaces to every member. How sparkly special would our routines be then?"

Wanda didn't disagree, so Pearl turned to Rocky. "You could buy your very own Shell Wars team! Or an entire zoo of friends for Zollie!" Zollie was Rocky's pet sea horse. "Plus, we'll get our pictures in the *Trident City Tide*! We'll be famous. Everyone will think we're the bravest merkids in all of Trident City!"

Rocky and Wanda were quiet for a minute. Finally they both nodded. "All right," Rocky said. "I'll do it for Zollie."

"And I'll do it for the Tail Flippers!" added Wanda.

Pearl grinned. "That's the spirit! Let's go." She floated up, up, and over the top of the ship.

"Ooooooooooooooooohhhhhhhh!"

Pearl froze at the sound, then gulped and looked behind her. Where were Wanda and Rocky?

She peered over the side of the ship and saw the two merkids hiding behind a large cup coral. "Come on, you scaredy slugs!" Pearl yelled.

Rocky's eyes were wide with fright. "That doesn't sound like rotting wood to me," he said. "It sounds like ghosts!"

Pearl couldn't believe that Rocky of all merkids was scared to explore the ship. He was always bragging about being brave. Plus, he was still wearing his pirate costume! Weren't pirates supposed to be fearless? Some pirate he turned out to be! "Well, forget them!"

Pearl whispered. "If they don't come, that just means more treasure for me!" She took a deep breath and disappeared into the belly of the dark ship.

Trapped

IT WAS SO DARK INSIDE THE SHIP that Pearl could barely see her hand in front of her face. Why hadn't she thought to bring a glowing phosphorescent jellyfish to help light the way? Still, it was thrilling. "I can't believe I'm in a pirate ship!" she exclaimed. She floated through what looked like storage rooms filled with shelves and old cabinets, but she didn't see any treasure.

"They probably kept the valuables, like jewels, deeper in the ship," she told herself as she glided through a trapdoor. She saw some pots and pans and figured this must have been the kitchen. Then again, she wasn't even sure if humans needed kitchens.

She saw a small light through a doorway and raced ahead, hoping it was the treasure chest. But it was just the glowing blue-green lure of another blackdevil fish. "Ew!" Pearl snapped. "You're a creepy-looking fish!"

She swam in between broken boards and cracked barrels. The water grew much colder as a bad feeling crept over her. She gulped and tried not to think that dead pirates could be watching her. She didn't want to be scared, so she got mad instead.

"I hate this!" Pearl muttered to a deep-sea angler that floated past her. "I like pretty rooms—not ones that are broken, splintered, and smashed. This isn't exciting at all!" She looked everywhere as she hurried through another storage room, but didn't see anything that looked like a pirate's treasure chest. All around her the wooden walls were encrusted with thousands of round adult barnacles. She couldn't help wondering why humans needed so many containers and coils of rope.

Pearl floated around the rusty barrel of

a human cannon, just like one she'd seen at the People Museum, and through a small hole in one of the ship's walls. Something sparkled up ahead. "I bet those are the jewels!" she exclaimed. "Wanda and Rocky are going to be sorry they were so scared!" Pearl's mind raced as she thought of all the things she could do with the jewels.

She had to wiggle through one more hole and the treasure would be hers! But when she tried to glide through it, her tail fin got caught. Pearl pulled and pulled, but it was no use! "Help! Help! I'm stuck!" she yelped. Tears welled in her eyes. The hole was pinching her tail!

Once again the ghostly sound echoed throughout the ship:

"Ooooooooooooooooohhhhhhhh!"

"Oh no!" Pearl wiggled. She tugged. She jerked, but it was no use. She was totally, completely stuck! "What was I thinking?" she moaned. "I shouldn't have come here without my parents. What if I'm trapped forever?"

She would have started crying, but a common fangtooth darted toward her, baring its huge, saberlike teeth. Instead of crying, Pearl yelled even louder for help. "Rocky! Wanda! Help meeeee! I'm stuck!"

Luckily, the fangtooth was frightened off by her screaming. Pearl shivered, then listened for Wanda and Rocky. Hadn't they heard her? "Help!" Pearl hollered again, but still no one came. Then she started to really worry. What if Rocky and Wanda had left? What if she was stuck and all alone?

8

Diamonds?

IN A FEW MINUTES, PEARL'S WORRY turned to anger. She was still stuck, and her throat was sore from yelling. But did Rocky and Wanda come to her rescue? No! Some friend Wanda turned out to be. "Didn't I help her when she was too scared to sleep in the same room as Kiki's skeleton bed?"

Pearl thought back to when Wanda had shared a dorm room with Kiki. Kiki slept in a horrible bed made from a killer whale's skeleton. The bed terrified Wanda, so Pearl had fixed it so that Kiki and her whale bed got a room of their own—away from Wanda. But now that Pearl needed help, where was Wanda? "She's probably having a sea cucumber snack at the Big Rock Café with Rocky!"

Pearl shook her tail hard, but it still didn't come loose. "They're having treats and I'm starving! I didn't even get an after-school snack. And with me gone, Wanda will probably try to steal my place on the Tail Flippers team!" Pearl had been sorry that Wanda hadn't made the team, but now she wasn't. The more she thought about it, the madder she got.

A baby octopus floated past her. "I guess I'm going to have to get *myself* out of this mess!" she hissed at the octopus, and angrily jerked her tail. It loosened just a tiny bit. Pearl closed her eyes and yanked with all her might. *Whoosh!* This time she tumbled away from the small hole.

She was free! Pearl carefully felt all around her fins, not really believing her good luck, then sighed with relief. She was loose and there wasn't a scratch on her.

She thought about heading home, but only for a second. The treasure chest was just too tempting. She had to have those jewels!

Pearl floated through a larger hole, toward the faint glow ahead. The closer she got, the more it sparkled. "It must be diamonds!" she cheered. Maybe her day

was turning around after all! Now she'd have the most fabulous story to tell the class tomorrow—and a necklace made of diamonds and rubies, too!

But when she got closer, Pearl saw neither diamonds nor rubies. In fact, there wasn't a treasure at all. The glow was coming from a large bed of bioluminescent plankton. The tiny sea creatures sparkled, but they weren't a treasure. "No!" Pearl shrieked. She had never been so disappointed.

Just then she heard the ghostly sound again.

"Oooooooooooooooooohhhhhhhh!"

The sound was so close that it made the water around her vibrate. Pearl knew she should dart home as fast as she could, but she had come too far not to find out what was making that sound. Was it really a ghost? And if so, was it guarding the treasure?

"Oooooooooooooooooohhhhhhhh!" The sound seemed to be coming from behind a metal door. The door creaked as Pearl pushed it open and swam inside a dark room.

"ARRGH!" A huge blast of water sent her plummeting backward.

"Oh no!" she shrieked. What was that? The pirate ghost?

Rescue

SO THAT'S THE PIRATE GHOST! Pearl thought. She hadn't really believed there was one, but now she'd seen it with her own eyes. Only it wasn't a pirate and it wasn't a ghost.

It was a giant octopus—the biggest one she'd ever seen. In the brief second she had glimpsed the octopus, Pearl noticed two things. One, the octopus was pale pink—almost white. Pearl knew from a recent lesson that they became white when they were hurt or in trouble. Of course, the second thing she'd noticed was that the octopus was stuck. Trapped—just like she had been!

"Ooooooooooooooooohhhhhhhh!" the octopus wailed.

"It's calling for help, just like I did," Pearl said. Should she help it? She was pretty sure octopuses didn't eat mermaids, and she'd never heard of a mermaid being killed by an octopus. And besides, maybe the giant creature was sitting on the treasure!

With a quick flip of her tail, she did the unthinkable. Pearl parted the water with her arms and came face-to-face with the enormous octopus.

Somehow one of the octopus's arms had gotten tangled in a coil of rusty wire. Pearl knew that just one of its long arms could squeeze her to death, but that didn't stop her. She was feeling very brave, and the treasure might be close at hand!

"Um . . . hi!" Pearl squeaked. She pulled on the wire, but it wouldn't budge. Then she tried to unwind the coil from the octopus's leg, but the wire was so stiff that she could barely move it. She needed something stronger; something that would slice right through it! But what?

Pearl glided back to the metal doorway. "Ooooooooooooooooohhhhhhhh!"

She stared at the octopus. "Don't worry. I'll be back. I have to find something to break that wire." She wasn't sure if the octopus understood or not, but it blinked one of its huge eyes.

Pearl swam through the doorway and searched all around for something to cut the wire. "Where's a sawfish when you need one?" she muttered. "A diamond would work too." After all, Mrs. Karp had said that diamonds were used for cutting doors in shells.

But Pearl couldn't find a sawfish or

a diamond. What was she going to do? She couldn't just leave the octopus, like Wanda and Rocky had left her. She had to help!

Just then something grabbed her from behind and jerked her around.

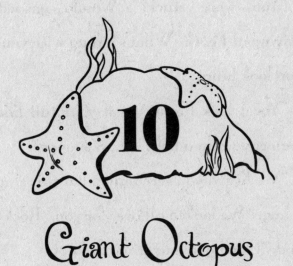

Giant Octopus

AAAAH!" PEARL SCREAMED.

"I guess we scared you," Rocky said with a smile. Wanda giggled nervously beside him.

Pearl didn't think it was funny at all. "Where have you been?" she demanded, her green eyes flashing with anger. "Why didn't you help me when I was stuck?"

"You were stuck?" Wanda gasped, staring at Pearl. "What's wrong with you? You look funny."

"You'd look funny too if your tail had been caught in a hole!" Pearl snapped.

"We heard you screaming, but this ship is huge! We looked all over for you," Rocky said. "Don't get your tail in a knot."

Even though she was mad they hadn't rescued her, Pearl was still hopeful that they had found the treasure. "Did you find anything?"

Rocky shook his head, causing his pirate hat to tilt slightly. "No, we were too busy looking for you! We didn't find anything except some peanut worms."

"Which he ate!" Wanda said, rolling her eyes.

"Hey, what can I say? I was hungry!" Rocky said with a grin, patting his stomach.

Pearl studied Rocky's pirate costume. She still couldn't believe how silly he looked. Then her eyes landed on the needlefish, and an idea popped into her head.

Pearl pulled the needlefish from Rocky's worm belt. "I need to borrow this," she called as she zoomed toward the metal doorway.

"Hey, that's mine!" Rocky cried, starting to follow her.

"I need it to—" Pearl said from the doorway, but the octopus interrupted her.

"Ooooooooooooooooooohhhhhhhh!"

"Whoa!" Rocky yelled, skidding to a stop. "Get away from that door. The pirate ghosts are in there!"

Pearl shook her head. "There are no pirate ghosts."

"Ooooooooooooooooooohhhhhhhh!"

"Pearl, don't go in there," Wanda said in a trembling voice.

"Ooooooooooooooooooohhhhhhhh!"

"Let's get out of here!" Rocky yelled. In two merseconds, he and Wanda had zoomed away.

"Stop!" Pearl shrieked, but they didn't even look back. They were so terrified that they didn't seem to realize she wasn't with them.

"They left me!" Pearl couldn't believe it. Well, she'd show them! She would save the octopus's life and find the treasure, too.

She swam into the room with the octopus and hacked at the wire with the needlefish's long, thick snout. Nothing happened.

"Ooooooooooooooooooohhhhhhhh!" the octopus moaned. Pearl hoped she wasn't hurting the octopus. She knew the needlefish's snout was very tough. Her father said it was strong enough to poke a hole in a boat.

"Rocky, get back here and help me!" Pearl cried. But Rocky didn't come back and neither did Wanda.

Pearl sniffed and kept chopping away. The whole time she muttered, "I wanted a chest full of sparkling jewels and all I found is an icky, nasty, and disgusting ship! This is the worst treasure hunt ever." Luckily, the wire was rusted and with one final whack, it broke.

"WEEEEoooooooooooooohhhhhhhh!" With a groan and a huge *whoosh*, the octopus exploded through the wall of the ship, sending pieces of wood flying in every direction.

Pearl ducked to avoid a big board. "How rude! That octopus didn't even thank me!" With the octopus gone, Pearl searched the room for any hint of the treasure. But it only had junk and not one single jewel.

This day had been one of the worst in the history of the ocean! She'd gotten stuck.

Her friends hadn't helped her. And to top it all off, there was no treasure! That meant no headline in the *Trident City Tide*. No diamond necklace for her story tomorrow! Could things get any worse?

11

Trouble

ROCKY AND WANDA WERE LONG gone. There was nothing for Pearl to do but head home. By the time she got back to her shell, she was too tired to move. Mrs. Swamp was waiting at the doorway, angrily thumping her tail. "Where have you been?" her mother demanded as Pearl slowly swam inside. "I was about to call the shark patrol on you!"

Before Pearl could answer, her mother gasped. "Why are you purple?"

"What?" Pearl screamed. She soared over to the massive mirror in the hallway and peeked at her reflection. It was true. Her face was purple! Her hands were purple. Her hair was purple. Even her beautiful pearls were purple!

The octopus! Its ink must have stained her completely and totally purple! Pearl knew that octopuses sometimes sprayed ink when they were scared. This was the only thanks she had gotten for saving a trapped creature. Pearl couldn't help it. She burst into tears.

Her mother wrapped her up in a big
hug. "Don't worry, angelfish. We'll get you
scrubbed up in no time."

Within two tail shakes, Pearl was soaking in a mixture of sea foam and coconut milk. After a couple of hours, the color had faded to a pale pinkish purple. She was dogfish worn out, *and* she still had to work on her story for tomorrow.

She sighed and tried to look on the bright side. At least she had an adventure to tell the class, even if it hadn't ended the way she'd hoped.

Her dad stopped her in the hallway as she was floating back to her room. "Young merlady, you are in big trouble," he thundered. "If I ever hear about you going to that pirate ship again, you will be grounded for the rest of your merlife!"

How had her dad found out? Rocky

must have told someone! Pearl didn't even try to deny it. She just sadly nodded and went to her room. After the disaster of a day—and no jewels—she hoped she didn't have any more adventures for a long time.

THE NEXT MORNING BEFORE CLASS, Headmaster Hermit's voice blared over the conch shell. "Pearl Swamp, come to the entrance hall."

Pearl gulped. Had he heard about her pirate adventures? What would the headmaster do? Maybe Echo was right and there was a rule against treasure hunting.

Pearl floated slowly toward Trident Academy's huge front hallway. Usually she liked looking at the colorful carvings on the ceiling, but not today. She was too afraid of getting kicked out of school. It was a big honor to go to the prestigious Trident Academy. What would her parents do if the headmaster told her she couldn't come anymore?

Headmaster Hermit stood in the middle of the grand hall with his arms folded over his chest. His black tail pounded the marble floor.

"D-d-did you want to see me?" Pearl asked in a shaky voice. Her mouth felt like it was full of sand!

The headmaster nodded. "You have a delivery, Miss Swamp."

"A delivery?" Pearl said in disbelief.

"Yes," Headmaster Hermit said with a frown. "In the future, please make sure all packages are sent to your shell. I will have Mr. Fangtooth deliver it there after school."

As he stepped aside, Pearl couldn't believe what she saw. There in the center of the hall was a treasure chest!

"But where? W-who?" Pearl stammered.

"A very large octopus dropped it off just a few minutes ago," Headmaster Hermit replied. "I tried to explain that you didn't live here, but my octopus language skills are somewhat . . . er . . . rusty." The headmaster looked a bit embarrassed and cleared his throat. "Nevertheless, let's make sure this doesn't happen again."

"Yes, sir," Pearl said, her eyes glued to the treasure chest.

"Now, get to class," Headmaster Hermit commanded.

Pearl scooted to her classroom, but all morning she had trouble concentrating on what Mrs. Karp was saying. Finally, just before lunch, it was time for everyone to share the stories they had made up. When the time came to tell her story, Pearl fumbled with the words.

"Yesterday, I mean once upon a time, a brave and beautiful mermaid went on a trip . . . a quest to find treasure on a haunted ship—a pirate ship. She got, er, stuck and her friends didn't help her."

Pearl glared at Rocky and Wanda before

continuing. "But she was so courageous that she escaped, rescued an octopus, and was rewarded with treasure!"

"That's not true!" Rocky blurted.

"Rocky," Mrs. Karp snapped. "This is Pearl's story, and she can tell it in any way she wants."

Pearl didn't mind. "It's all true! And it happened to me! If you don't believe me, just go look in the front hallway," she said, smugly tossing her blond hair behind her. "The treasure chest is there right now!"

The whole classroom erupted in excited chatter. Mrs. Karp held up her hand. "Pearl, are you making this up?" she asked sternly.

Pearl shook her head. "No, Mrs. Karp.

There really is a treasure chest in Trident Academy's front hall. And it's all mine!"

Mrs. Karp peered over her glasses at Pearl. "Well, students, I think we are all curious. Shall we float over to the front entrance to see this chest?"

Everyone lined up faster than a lizard-fish can catch its dinner. "She's telling a whopper of a lie," Rocky told the class.

But when they got to the front hallway, everyone was quiet. Even Pearl. Because there was no treasure chest. The hallway was completely empty!

A Real Treasure

WHAT HAPPENED TO IT? It was right here!" Pearl blurted out.

"Sure it was," Rocky said, scrunching his nose.

"But it really *was* here just a merminute

ago!" Pearl told the class desperately. "Ask Headmaster Hermit!"

Wanda shook her head. "Rocky and I were with Pearl yesterday, and we never saw an octopus."

"That's because you left me!" Pearl screeched.

Wanda's face turned bright red. "I'm sorry, but we thought you were with us."

"Yeah," Rocky chimed in. "And there was definitely no treasure. Pearl is telling a big lie."

"There was too, and I am not!" Pearl yelled. She couldn't believe they would accuse her of lying!

Mrs. Karp shook her head. "We've wasted enough time with this treasure chest business. Let's get back to class."

Pearl dragged her tail back to their room. The rest of the kids floated slowly too. No one was in a hurry to get back to schoolwork. In the hallway, Echo tried to cheer Pearl up. "Don't worry about it. You certainly made the morning more exciting."

"You don't believe me, do you?" Pearl asked Echo.

"Well . . . ," Echo said slowly.

"Maybe you just got carried away with your story," Shelly said quickly.

Kiki nodded. "Like when you said you have ten mirrors at home. Maybe you exaggerated just a bit."

Pearl angrily swished her tail. "But we *do* have ten mirrors at home! And I'm *not* pretending! Headmaster Hermit showed me the treasure. He said that Mr. Fangtooth would take it to my shell after school." She paused, then smiled. "That's it!"

"What's it?" Rocky asked as he swam over.

"I bet Mr. Fangtooth moved it out of the way to keep it safe."

Rocky groaned. "Why don't you just admit that you made the whole thing up?"

"But I didn't," Pearl insisted. "I'll show you after school at my shell."

"Forget it!" Rocky said. Kiki, Shelly, and Echo shook their heads. Even Wanda, who floated nearby, didn't look so sure.

Pearl felt so defeated! How could she prove that there really was a treasure? "Okay, fine," she said, crossing her arms.

"Come with me at lunchtime to find the chest, and I'll share a piece of the treasure with each of you."

Rocky grinned. "*Now* you're talking."

AT LUNCHTIME, PEARL LED ROCKY, Echo, Shelly, Wanda, and Kiki down a side hallway to Mr. Fangtooth's office. "It's got to be in here," Pearl told them.

"If Mr. Fangtooth catches us, we'll be in big trouble," Echo whispered.

"Why?" Pearl said. "It's my property, after all. A giant octopus gave it to me as a reward for saving his life."

"For real?" Kiki said.

"You actually saved an octopus?" Shelly asked.

Pearl nodded and pushed open a dark seaweed curtain. Quietly the six kids swam into Mr. Fangtooth's office.

"Look!" Wanda squealed. "There really is a treasure chest!"

"Wow!" Kiki exclaimed. The kids floated around an old black trunk with a rounded top, staring in wonder.

Pearl smiled. "See, I told you I was telling the truth."

"So did you really save an octopus too?" Echo asked.

"It even squirted me with ink," Pearl said, holding up her pinkish-purple arms.

"Oh my goodness, you *are* kind of purple," Shelly admitted. Pearl frowned. She wasn't happy about being purple, but it did prove that she was telling the truth.

"That was brave, Pearl," Echo said, and everyone else nodded their heads.

"You're a real explorer!" Shelly said, clearly impressed.

"But what's inside the chest?" Wanda asked.

Pearl's eyes lit up. "I don't know, but we're about to find out."

"Don't forget," Rocky reminded her. "You promised all of us a piece of the treasure."

Pearl wished she hadn't said that, but a promise was a promise. She put her hand on the chest's lid and tugged. It wouldn't open. She pulled harder.

"Let's help," Shelly suggested. So the merkids grabbed the lid and pulled together.

They all fell backward when the lid popped open.

"Is it full of diamonds and rubies?" Wanda asked.

Pearl was the first to look inside. She shrieked.

"What is it?" Echo asked. "Emeralds and sapphires?"

All the merkids crowded around to see inside. Pink and yellow jewels glittered in front of them.

"It's jewels, all right," Rocky said, laughing. "Jewel anemones!"

Pearl felt like crying. She'd risked her life on an old pirate ship—all for some silly coral-like animals. Where were the jewels? Where were the diamonds and rubies?

There was a long silence. Finally Shelly spoke up, "Pearl, these are actually a very rare type of jewel anemone. I bet the octopus thought they *were* valuable."

Pearl groaned. No matter what Shelly said, a few boring anemones were nothing like diamonds and rubies! They most certainly wouldn't bring her any fame or fortune.

"Look at it this way: There may not have been a treasure inside this chest," Shelly continued, "but you have to admit you brought a lot of excitement to Trident Academy."

Kiki nodded. "Plus, if it wasn't for you, the octopus would still be stuck. Maybe helping others is more important than jewels."

Pearl considered this. She still wished she had some real treasure, but she did have an adventure that definitely wasn't boring. And she'd rescued an octopus, just like a real hero. So she shrugged. "I guess I *am* pretty exciting."

"In fact," Wanda said with a grin, "I think you're Trident Academy's own secret treasure."

Class Stories

★ ✦ ★

PETUNIA THE PIRATE

By Shelly Siren

Petunia was a pirate with a secret. She was scared of water. She even hated when she had to wash the deck of the ship. But something happened to make her love the water. Can you guess what it was?

PATTY-CAKE THE PIRATE

By Echo Reef

Once there was a pirate who liked to play games. He played Shell Wars. He played human games. But the game he liked best was patty-cake. Once, he started playing it and couldn't stop! Finally the other pirates on his ship couldn't stand it and tossed him overboard. If you listen closely to the ocean, you can still hear him slapping the water with his hands, playing patty-cake.

DREADLY, THE DREADED PIRATE

By Rocky Ridge

Everyone dreaded Dreadly, the Dreaded Pirate. He was mean and scary and had only one eye. A shark had stolen the other one. Dreadly hated sharks and hunted them when he wasn't swiping treasure. Once, Dreadly found the biggest shark ever, Enormo Shark. Dreadly was going to kill it. Enormo Shark told Dreadly, the Dreaded Pirate, that he hadn't taken his eye. Dreadly wouldn't listen, so Enormo

Shark ate Dreadly. That was the end of Dreadly—except for his eyeball. If you ever see a shark with three eyes, that's the one that took Dreadly's eyeball.

PEARL THE PIRATE
By Pearl Swamp

Yesterday, I mean once upon a time, a brave and beautiful mermaid went on a trip . . . a quest to find treasure on a haunted ship—a pirate ship. She got stuck and her friends didn't help her. But she was so courageous that she escaped, rescued an octopus, and was rewarded with treasure!

GOOD PIRATES
By Kiki Coral

Did you know there are still pirates today? Most people think they were from long ago, but human ships are still being attacked. One of my brothers told me about one where the pirates held the people hostage. He thought about helping them, but some other humans in funny green clothes came and took the ship away from the bad pirates. The humans in those funny green clothes must be good pirates.

The Mermaid Song

REFRAIN:

Let the water roar

Deep down we're swimming along

Twirling, swirling, singing the mermaid song.

VERSE 1:

Shelly flips her tail

Racing, diving, chasing a whale

Twirling, swirling, singing the mermaid song.

VERSE 2:

Pearl likes to shine

Oh my Neptune, she looks so fine

Twirling, swirling, singing the mermaid song.

VERSE 3:

Shining Echo flips her tail

Backward and forward without fail

Twirling, swirling, singing the mermaid song.

VERSE 4:

Amazing Kiki

Far from home and floating so free

Twirling, swirling, singing the mermaid song.

Author's Note

YOU MAY HAVE GUESSED THAT I think writing stories is exciting. And telling those stories out loud can be even more fun. In fact, I love hearing old family stories around the kitchen table. The best ones start with "Do you remember when . . ." Many stories that have been passed down for hundreds of years probably started just that way. Can you remember something funny that happened at your school or at home? Try

★ 99 ★

writing it down. Then practice telling it at the dinner table. You may have started a story that will be told for hundreds of years! I hope you'll visit my website for more writing fun at www.debbiedadey.com.

Swim free,
Debbie Dadey

Glossary

ACORN BARNACLE: The adult acorn barnacle fixes itself to one spot using a cementlike substance.

ANGELFISH: The queen angelfish is one of the most colorful of the Caribbean reef fish. The adults are blue and yellow, but younger fish are brown and yellow.

BIOLUMINESCENT PLANKTON: This tiny organism makes bright flashes of light. In large groups, they make glowing seas.

BLACKDEVIL FISH: The common blackdevil

is a deep-sea fish with a glowing lure and long, sharp teeth.

BLACK DRAGONFISH: The Pacific black dragonfish is a creepy bottom dweller with dagger-sharp teeth and glowing photophores on its belly.

BOOTLACE WORM: This very skinny worm is one of the longest animals known. It can get up to thirty-three feet long. Most people can't throw a ball that far.

COFFINFISH: This fish looks more like a pink balloon than a coffin!

COMMON FANGTOOTH: The huge spikelike teeth of this fish give it a scary look!

CREEPING COMB JELLY: The creeping comb jelly is a bottom dweller and lives on the orange sea star.

CONCH: This is a common name for the large spiral shell of a sea snail.

CUP CORAL: The Devonshire cup coral attaches to a rock or shipwreck and is cup-shaped.

CUTTLEFISH: The Australian giant cuttlefish is the largest of the one hundred kinds of cuttlefish. It grows up to five feet and resembles an octopus.

DEAD MAN'S FINGERS: This soft coral does look a bit like stubby fingers!

DOGFISH: The piked dogfish is actually a shark. It is very slow growing and can live to be one hundred years old.

GOBLIN SHARK: The goblin shark should be called the unicorn shark because of its pointed snout.

JELLYFISH: The moon jellyfish can be found in almost every part of the ocean. It is shaped like a small saucer with fine tentacles, like fringe, hanging from it. The upside-down jellyfish is often mistaken for being dead. Some jellyfish actually glow!

JEWEL ANEMONES: Jewel anemones sometimes live on underwater cliffs and create a beautiful display when grouped together. They can be almost any color, but often appear as yellow and pink.

KELP: Kelp is large brown seaweed. Sea otters often live in undersea kelp forests.

KILLER WHALE: This is the largest member of the dolphin family.

LANTERNFISH: The spotted lanternfish is a small fish that can put on a fabulous light display from the photophores along its sides and belly.

LIZARDFISH: The reef lizardfish darts out from its perch on rocks or corals to seize a fish for dinner. Its large mouth lets it swallow quite large fish.

MANTA RAY: This huge ray can leap out of the water and is known to be friendly with divers.

MOLLUSKS: This group of marine animals includes oysters, sea slugs, and octopuses.

MOTHER-OF-PEARL: Mother of pearl, or nacre, is the inside layer of pearl oyster shells.

NEEDLEFISH: Most people don't like to eat the hound needlefish because its flesh is green.

OCTOPUS: The blue-ringed octopus lives in

the tropical Pacific and Indian Oceans. Its spit can kill a human!

PEARL: Pearls are actually formed inside an oyster!

PEANUT WORM: This bottom-living creature looks more like a sausage than a peanut.

SAWFISH: The endangered smalltooth saw-fish is a ray with a long, flat, sawlike snout.

SEA APPLE: The sea apple has a red and purple body and is often used in aquariums because it is so colorful.

SEA CUCUMBER: This animal crawls along the bottom of the sea, sucking up sediment as it moves along.

SEA HORSE: The pygmy sea horse is a minia-ture sea horse that hides in tiny sea fan coral.

SEA PEN: The slender sea pen grows on the

bottom of sheltered sea lochs near Scotland and Norway. It resembles a feather in appearance.

SEA SLUG: The bright color and bad taste of the Chromodoris sea slug protects it from predators.

SEAWEED: Seaweed is used for food, cosmetics, medicine, fertilizer, and even in beer!

SHARK: The whale shark is the largest fish in the world. Its mouth is so big, a human could fit inside. Luckily, it eats only plankton and small fish.

TOADFISH: If you hear a loud grunting noise along the water, it just might be an oyster toadfish.

VAMPIRE SQUIDS: These squids live at the bottom of the ocean and have light organs on the tips of their arms.

WHALES: The blue whale is probably the biggest animal that has ever lived. Its call is louder than the sound a jet airplane makes when it takes off! (It is not a fish.)

WRECKFISH: This large fish often lurks in wrecked sunken ships.

ZOANTHID: White zoanthids love to cover rocks, wrecks, and even worm tubes.

FIND OUT WHAT HAPPENS IN THE NEXT . . .

Mermaid Tales

Debbie Dadey

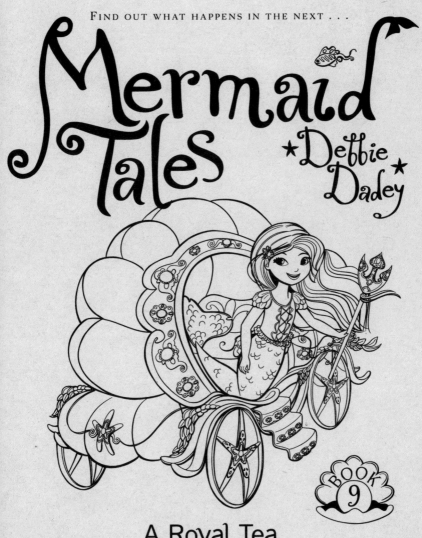

BOOK 9

A Royal Tea

Holiday?

"S HELLY!" MRS. KARP SAID. "WHAT are you doing here?"

Shelly Siren looked around her third-grade classroom in surprise. It was first thing in the morning at her school, Trident Academy, and the other mer-students were just settling into their desks.

"It's Wednesday," Shelly told her teacher. "It isn't a holiday, is it?"

A merboy named Rocky Ridge swam out of his rock desk toward the classroom doorway. "Holiday? All right! I'm going home!"

Mrs. Karp slapped her white tail on her marble desk. "Not so fast, young merman. It's not a holiday."

Rocky groaned, but Shelly was relieved. She had been afraid she had come to school on the wrong day. Things had been a little mixed up at her shell lately.

"I heard your grandfather has penguin pox, Shelly, and I know it's highly contagious," Mrs. Karp said with a worried look on her face, "so I wasn't sure if you'd be at school today."

"Penguin pox? Eek!" Several kids in the classroom pushed their desks away from Shelly.

Pearl Swamp put her hands over her nose and squealed, "Mrs. Karp, get her out of here right now before we all die!"

Mrs. Karp frowned. "Pearl, you can't die from penguin pox."

"Maybe not," Rocky said. "But you do get itchy black-and-white bumps all over your body."

"Don't worry." Echo Reef put her arm around Shelly. "She isn't sick." Echo was Shelly's best friend.

Shelly nodded, causing her red hair to swirl in the water around her. "My grand-father became ill after he visited a museum in far-off waters. He's locked away with a nurse to take care of him so I don't catch it. I haven't even seen him in days." Shelly's parents had died when she was very young, so she lived with her grandfather.

"I'm glad you're healthy, Shelly. And I hope your grandfather is well soon too," Mrs. Karp said, turning her attention back to the class. "All right, then. Let's all take our seats and get to work. Today we are starting a new unit on penguins!"

Kiki Coral, the smallest mergirl in the class, leaned over and patted Shelly's hand. "I'm sorry about your grandfather. I hope he gets better soon."

Shelly nodded and tried to listen to the science lesson, but she found it hard to concentrate on her favorite subject. Everyone in the merclass, except for Kiki and Echo, kept their desks scooted far away. They even tucked their tails in tightly beneath them so that they wouldn't accidentally touch Shelly. Pearl held her nose whenever she looked at Shelly. No one wanted to catch the penguin pox!

Shelly felt awful. Why was everyone acting like she had a horrible disease? She was almost glad when Rocky yelled, "Mrs. Karp, look! I need to go home. I have the dreaded penguin pox!"

Everyone in the class gasped, but Shelly knew the spots on Rocky's arms were fake. She'd watched him draw them on with a sea quill and octopus ink.

Mrs. Karp rushed over to Rocky, took one look at the pretend spots, and pointed to the hallway. "Mr. Ridge, please step outside for a little conference."

"Ooh," several merboys in the room howled as Rocky slowly followed Mrs. Karp out of the classroom.

"Look at what you've done," Pearl snapped at Shelly. "You've gotten poor Rocky into trouble with your icky disease!"

Poor Rocky? Since when did Pearl care about anyone but herself? Shelly sighed. She had a feeling that this wasn't the end of her penguin pox problems.

Debbie Dadey

is the author and coauthor of more than one hundred and fifty children's books, including the series The Adventures of the Bailey School Kids. A former teacher and librarian, Debbie now lives in Bucks County, Pennsylvania, with her wonderful husband, three children, and three dogs. She recently went to Jamaica and thought she saw a mermaid there! If you see any mermaids, let her know at www.debbiedadey.com.

Candy Fairies

Chocolate Dreams

Rainbow Swirl

Caramel Moon

Cool Mint

Magic Hearts

Gooey Goblins

The Sugar Ball

A Valentine's
Surprise

Bubble Gum
Rescue

Double Dip

Jelly Bean Jumble

The Chocolate
Rose

A Royal Wedding

Marshmallow
Mystery

Frozen Treats

The Sugar Cup

Sweet Secrets

Taffy Trouble

Visit candyfairies.com
for games, recipes, and more!